Fantasies, Preludes, Fugues
and Other Works for Organ

MAX REGER

Dover Publications, Inc.
New York

Bibliographical Note

This Dover edition, first published in 1995, is a new compilation of works originally published separately. All were designated "für Orgel." Rob. Forberg originally published *Phantasie und Fugue, Op. 29* (1899). Jos. Aibl Verlag, G.m.b.H., Leipzig, originally published three works in this collection: *Phantasie und Fuge über den Namen BACH*, Op. 46 (1900); *Variationen und Fuge über "Heil Unserem König, Heil"* (1901); and *Fünf leicht ausführbare Präludien und Fugen, Op. 56* (in two volumes) (1904). Ed. Bote & G. Bock, Berlin, originally published *Introduktion, Passacaglia und Fuge, Op. 127* (1913). *Suite*, Op. 92, and *Neun Stücke*, Op. 129, were originally published in authoritative German editions, n.d.

The Dover edition adds: a unified table of contents in English and German; a glossary of German terms used in these scores; and new headings throughout. New English translations accompany the original German footnotes on pp. 30 and 40.

International Standard Book Number: 0-486-28846-3

Manufactured in the United States of America
Dover Publications, Inc., 31 East 2nd Street, Mineola, N.Y. 11501

Contents

Glossary of German Terms   vii

Fantasy and Fugue, Op. 29 (composed 1898)

[Phantasie und Fuge]
Fantasy   2   •   *Fugue*   7

Fantasy and Fugue on the Name BACH, Op. 46 (1900)

[Phantasie und Fuge über den Namen BACH]
Fantasy   17   •   *Fugue*   30

Variations and Fugue on "God Save the King"
   [no opus number] (1901?)

[Variationen und Fuge über "Heil, Unserem König, Heil"]
Variations   43   •   *Fugue*   46

Five Easy Preludes and Fugues, Op. 56 (1904)

[Fünf leicht ausführbare Präludien und Fugen]
No. 1 in E Major: *Prelude*   52   •   *Fugue*   56
No. 2 in D Minor: *Prelude*   60   •   *Fugue*   65
No. 3 in G Major: *Prelude*   70   •   *Fugue*   74
No. 4 in C Major: *Prelude*   78   •   *Fugue*   81
No. 5 in B Minor: *Prelude*   84   •   *Fugue*   88

Suite, Op. 92 (1905)

1. Prelude [Präludium]   92
2. Fugue [Fuge]   96
3. Intermezzo   99
4. Basso ostinato   104
5. Romance [Romanze]   106
6. Toccata   110
7. Fugue [Fuge]   114

Introduction, Passacaglia and Fugue, Op. 127 (1913)

[Introduktion, Passacaglia und Fuge]

Introduction 119 • *Passacaglia* 124 • *Fugue* 147

Nine Pieces, Op. 129 (1913)

[Neun Stücke]

1. Toccata   165
2. Fugue [Fuge]   168
3. Canon [Kanon]   173
4. Melodia   176
5. Capriccio   178
6. Basso ostinato   183
7. Intermezzo   186
8. Prelude [Präludium]   188
9. Fugue [Fuge]   192

Glossary of German Terms

alle, all

etwas, rather, somewhat

hervortretend, prominent, to the fore

im, in the

nach und nach beschleunigen = *accelerando poco a poco*
nicht, not
nur, only

ohne, without

zart, subdued, gentle

Fantasies, Preludes, Fugues
and Other Works for Organ

Fantasy and Fugue

[*Phantasie und Fuge*]
Op. 29 (1898)

FANTASY

FUGUE

Respectfully dedicated to the Honorable Privy Councillor
Professor Dr. J. von Rheinberger

Fantasy and Fugue
on the Name BACH

[*Phantasie und Fuge über den Namen BACH*]
Op. 46 (1900)

FANTASY

Fantasy and Fugue on the Name BACH, Op. 46

Fantasy and Fugue on the Name BACH, Op. 46

FUGUE

a) Von [c - d] können die oberen Noten der linken Hand ausgelassen werden. (4⅔ Takte.)
[From c to d the upper notes in the left hand may be omitted (4⅔ measures).]

Variations and Fugue
on "God Save the King"

[Variationen und Fuge über "Heil, Unserem König, Heil"]

(1901?)

For Richard Braungart

Five Easy Preludes and Fugues

[*Fünf leicht ausführbare Präludien und Fugen*]
Op. 56 (1904)

I. PRELUDE and FUGUE in E MAJOR

Five Easy Preludes and Fugues, Op. 56

2. PRELUDE AND FUGUE IN D MINOR

Allegrissimo.

3. PRELUDE AND FUGUE IN G MAJOR

4. PRELUDE AND FUGUE IN C MAJOR

Five Easy Preludes and Fugues, OP. 56

5. PRELUDE AND FUGUE IN B MINOR

Moderato.

II. Man.(Sw.)

Suite
Op. 92 (1905)

I. PRELUDE

Andante con moto.

2. FUGUE

3. INTERMEZZO

Andante.

4. BASSO OSTINATO

5. ROMANCE

6. TOCCATA

110

Allegro moderato.

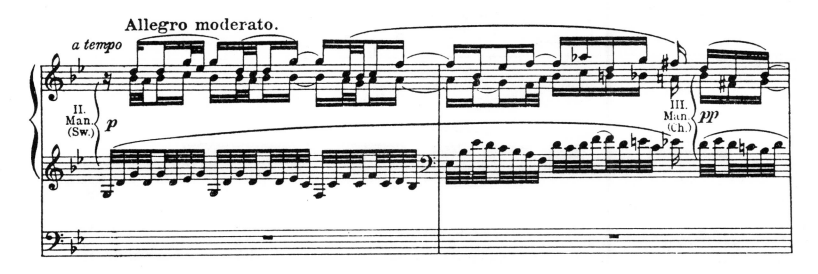

7. FUGUE

Introduction, Passacaglia and Fugue

[*Introduktion, Passacaglia und Fuge*]

Op. 127 (1913)

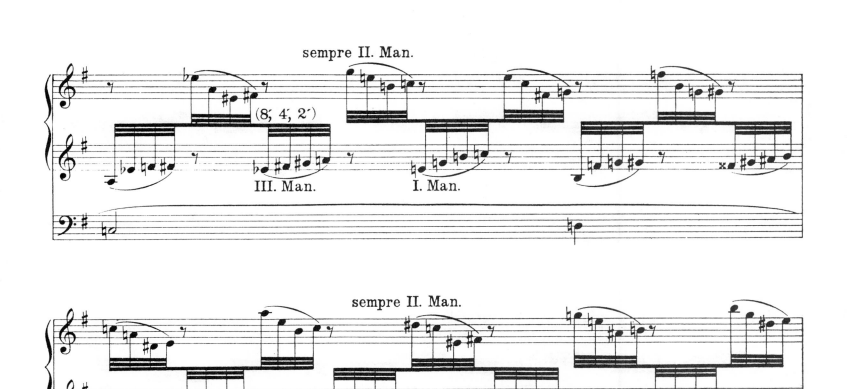

Introduction, Passacaglia and Fugue, Op. 127

Dedicated to my dear friend Hans von Ohlendorff

Nine Pieces

[*Neun Stücke*]

Op. 129 (1913)

I. TOCCATA

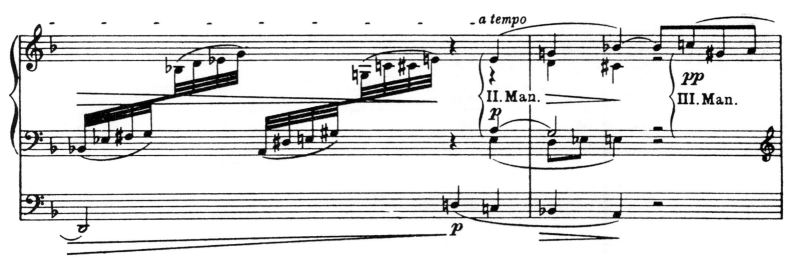

2. FUGUE

3. CANON

4. MELODIA

5. CAPRICCIO

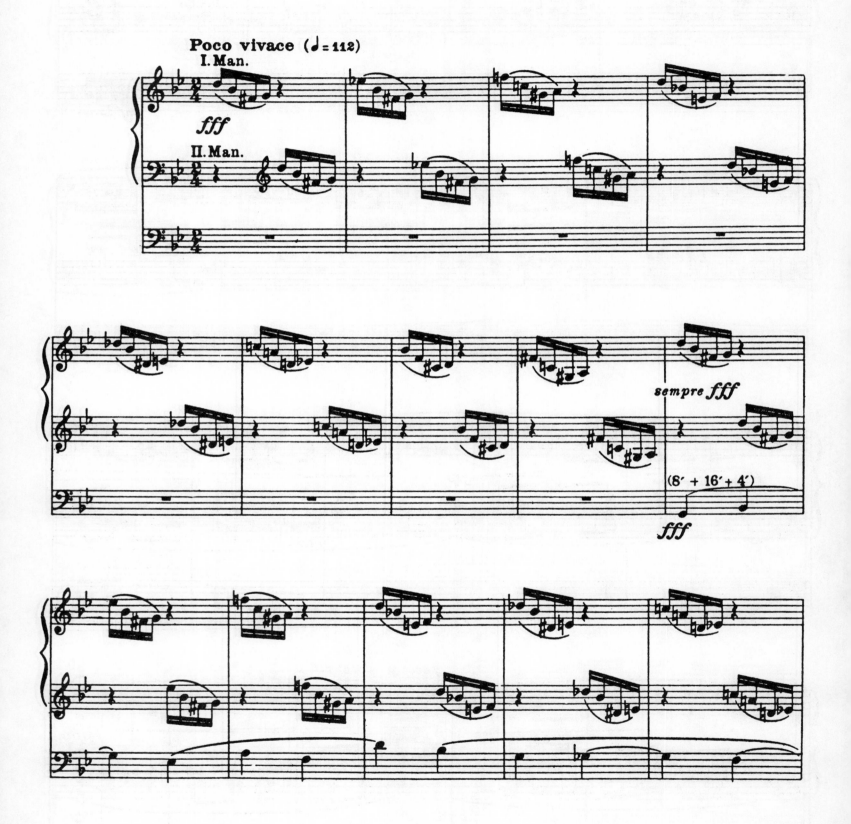

178

6. BASSO OSTINATO

7. INTERMEZZO

8. PRELUDE

9. FUGUE

END OF EDITION

Dover Piano and Keyboard Editions

THE WELL-TEMPERED CLAVIER: Books I and II, Complete, Johann Sebastian Bach. All 48 preludes and fugues in all major and minor keys. Authoritative Bach-Gesellschaft edition. Explanation of ornaments in English, tempo indications, music corrections. 208pp. 9⅜ × 12¼. 24532-2 Pa. **$9.95**

KEYBOARD MUSIC, J. S. Bach. Bach-Gesellschaft edition. For harpsichord, piano, other keyboard instruments. English Suites, French Suites, Six Partitas, Goldberg Variations, Two-Part Inventions, Three-Part Sinfonias. 312pp. 8⅛ × 11. 22360-4 Pa. **$10.95**

ITALIAN CONCERTO, CHROMATIC FANTASIA AND FUGUE AND OTHER WORKS FOR KEYBOARD, Johann Sebastian Bach. Sixteen of Bach's best-known, most-performed and most-recorded works for the keyboard, reproduced from the authoritative Bach-Gesellschaft edition. 112pp. 9 × 12. 25387-2 Pa. **$8.95**

COMPLETE KEYBOARD TRANSCRIPTIONS OF CONCERTOS BY BAROQUE COMPOSERS, Johann Sebastian Bach. Sixteen concertos by Vivaldi, Telemann and others, transcribed for solo keyboard instruments. Bach-Gesellschaft edition. 128pp. 9⅜ × 12¼. 25529-8 Pa. **$8.95**

ORGAN MUSIC, J. S. Bach. Bach-Gesellschaft edition. 93 works. 6 Trio Sonatas, German Organ Mass, Orgelbüchlein, Six Schubler Chorales, 18 Choral Preludes. 357pp. 8⅛ × 11. 22359-0 Pa. **$12.95**

COMPLETE PRELUDES AND FUGUES FOR ORGAN, Johann Sebastian Bach. All 25 of Bach's complete sets of preludes and fugues (i.e. compositions written as pairs), from the authoritative Bach-Gesellschaft edition. 168pp. 8⅜ × 11. 24816-X Pa. **$9.95**

TOCCATAS, FANTASIAS, PASSACAGLIA AND OTHER WORKS FOR ORGAN, J. S. Bach. Over 20 best-loved works including Toccata and Fugue in D minor, BWV 565; Passacaglia and Fugue in C minor, BWV 582, many more. Bach-Gesellschaft edition. 176pp. 9 × 12. 25403-8 Pa. **$9.95**

TWO- AND THREE-PART INVENTIONS, J. S. Bach. Reproduction of original autograph ms. Edited by Eric Simon. 62pp. 8⅛ × 11. 21982-8 Pa. **$7.95**

THE 36 FANTASIAS FOR KEYBOARD, Georg Philipp Telemann. Graceful compositions by 18th-century master. 1923 Breslauer edition. 80pp. 8⅛ × 11. 25365-1 Pa. **$5.95**

GREAT KEYBOARD SONATAS, Carl Philipp Emanuel Bach. Comprehensive two-volume edition contains 51 sonatas by second, most important son of Johann Sebastian Bach. Originality, rich harmony, delicate workmanship. Authoritative French edition. Total of 384pp. 8⅜ × 11¼. Series I 24853-4 Pa. **$9.95**
Series II 24854-2 Pa. **$9.95**

KEYBOARD WORKS/Series One: Ordres I-XIII; Series Two: Ordres XIV-XXVII and Miscellaneous Pieces, François Couperin. Over 200 pieces. Reproduced directly from edition prepared by Johannes Brahms and Friedrich Chrysander. Total of 496pp. 8⅛ × 11. Series I 25795-9 Pa. **$9.95**
Series II 25796-7 Pa. **$9.95**

KEYBOARD WORKS FOR SOLO INSTRUMENTS, G. F. Handel. 35 neglected works from Handel's vast oeuvre, originally jotted down as improvisations. Includes Eight Great Suites, others. New sequence. 174pp. 9⅜ × 12¼. 24338-9 Pa. **$9.95**

WORKS FOR ORGAN AND KEYBOARD, Jan Pieterszoon Sweelinck. Nearly all of early Dutch composer's difficult-to-find keyboard works. Chorale variations; toccatas, fantasias; variations on secular, dance tunes. Also, incomplete and/or modified works, plus fantasia by John Bull. 272pp. 9 × 12. 24935-2 Pa. **$11.95**

ORGAN WORKS, Dietrich Buxtehude. Complete organ works of extremely influential pre-Bach composer. Toccatas, preludes, chorales, more. Definitive Breitkopf & Härtel edition. 320pp. 8⅜ × 11¼. (Available in U.S. only) 25682-0 Pa. **$12.95**

THE FUGUES ON THE MAGNIFICAT FOR ORGAN OR KEYBOARD, Johann Pachelbel. 94 pieces representative of Pachelbel's magnificent contribution to keyboard composition; can be played on the organ, harpsichord or piano. 100pp. 9 × 12. (Available in U.S. only) 25037-7 Pa. **$7.95**

MY LADY NEVELLS BOOKE OF VIRGINAL MUSIC, William Byrd. 42 compositions in modern notation from 1591 ms. For any keyboard instrument. 245pp. 8⅛ × 11. 22246-2 Pa. **$13.95**

ELIZABETH ROGERS HIR VIRGINALL BOOKE, edited with calligraphy by Charles J. F. Cofone. All 112 pieces from noted 1656 manuscript, most never before published. Composers include Thomas Brewer, William Byrd, Orlando Gibbons, etc. 125pp. 9 × 12. 23138-0 Pa. **$10.95**

THE FITZWILLIAM VIRGINAL BOOK, edited by J. Fuller Maitland, W. B. Squire. Famous early 17th-century collection of keyboard music, 300 works by Morley, Byrd, Bull, Gibbons, etc. Modern notation. Total of 938pp. 8⅜ × 11. Two-vol. set. 21068-5, 21069-3 Pa. **$33.90**

GREAT KEYBOARD SONATAS, Series I and Series II, Domenico Scarlatti. 78 of the most popular sonatas reproduced from the G. Ricordi edition edited by Alessandro Longo. Total of 320pp. 8⅜ × 11¼. Series I 24996-4 Pa. **$7.95**
Series II 25003-2 Pa. **$8.95**

SONATAS AND FANTASIES FOR THE PIANO, W. A. Mozart, edited by Nathan Broder. Finest, most accurate edition, based on autographs and earliest editions. 19 sonatas, plus Fantasy and Fugue in C, K.394, Fantasy in C Minor, K.396, Fantasy in D Minor, K.397. 352pp. 9 × 12. (Available in U.S. only) 25417-8 Pa. **$16.50**

COMPLETE PIANO SONATAS, Joseph Haydn. 52 sonatas reprinted from authoritative Breitkopf & Härtel edition. Extremely clear and readable; ample space for notes, analysis. 464pp. 9⅜ × 12¼. 24726-0 Pa. **$10.95**
24727-9 Pa. **$10.95**

BAGATELLES, RONDOS AND OTHER SHORTER WORKS FOR PIANO, Ludwig van Beethoven. Most popular and most performed shorter works, including Rondo a capriccio in G and Andante in F. Breitkopf & Härtel edition. 128pp. 9⅜ × 12¼. 25392-9 Pa. **$8.95**

COMPLETE VARIATIONS FOR SOLO PIANO, Ludwig van Beethoven. Contains all 21 sets of Beethoven's piano variations, including the extremely popular *Diabelli Variations, Op. 120.* 240pp. 9⅜ × 12¼. 25188-8 Pa. **$11.95**

COMPLETE PIANO SONATAS, Ludwig van Beethoven. All sonatas in fine Schenker edition, with fingering, analytical material. One of best modern editions. 615pp. 9 × 12. Two-vol. set. 23134-8, 23135-6 Pa. **$23.90**

COMPLETE SONATAS FOR PIANOFORTE SOLO, Franz Schubert. All 15 sonatas. Breitkopf and Härtel edition. 293pp. 9⅜ × 12¼. 22647-6 Pa. **$13.95**

DANCES FOR SOLO PIANO, Franz Schubert. Over 350 waltzes, minuets, landler, ecossaises, other charming, melodic dance compositions reprinted from the authoritative Breitkopf & Härtel edition. 192pp. 9⅜ × 12¼. 26107-7 Pa. **$9.95**

*Available from your music dealer or write for **free** Music Catalog to Dover Publications, Inc., Dept. MUBI, 31 East 2nd Street, Mineola, N.Y. 11501.*

Dover Piano and Keyboard Editions

ORGAN WORKS, César Franck. Composer's best-known works for organ, including Six Pieces, Trois Pieces, and Trois Chorals. Oblong format for easy use at keyboard. Authoritative Durand edition. 208pp. 11⅜ × 8¼. 25517-4 Pa. **$10.95**

IBERIA AND ESPAÑA: Two Complete Works for Solo Piano, Isaac Albeniz. Spanish composer's greatest piano works in authoritative editions. Includes the popular "Tango". 192pp. 9 × 12. 25367-8 Pa. **$10.95**

GOYESCAS, SPANISH DANCES AND OTHER WORKS FOR SOLO PIANO, Enrique Granados. Great Spanish composer's most admired, most performed suites for the piano, in definitive Spanish editions. 176pp. 9 × 12. 25481-X Pa. **$8.95**

SELECTED PIANO COMPOSITIONS, César Franck, edited by Vincent d'Indy. Outstanding selection of influential French composer's piano works, including early pieces and the two masterpieces—Prelude, Choral and Fugue; and Prelude, Aria and Finale. Ten works in all. 138pp. 9 × 12. 23269-7 Pa. **$9.95**

THE COMPLETE PRELUDES AND ETUDES FOR PIANOFORTE SOLO, Alexander Scriabin. All the preludes and études including many perfectly spun miniatures. Edited by K. N. Igumnov and Y. I. Mil'shteyn. 250pp. 9 × 12. 22919-X Pa. **$10.95**

COMPLETE PIANO SONATAS, Alexander Scriabin. All ten of Scriabin's sonatas, reprinted from an authoritative early Russian edition. 256pp. 8⅜ × 11¼. 25850-5 Pa. **$10.95**

COMPLETE PRELUDES AND ETUDES-TABLEAUX, Serge Rachmaninoff. Forty-one of his greatest works for solo piano, including the riveting C minor, G-minor and B-minor preludes, in authoritative editions. 208pp. 8⅜ × 11¼. (Available in U.S. only) 25696-0 Pa. **$10.95**

COMPLETE PIANO SONATAS, Sergei Prokofiev. Definitive Russian edition of nine sonatas (1907–1953), among the most important compositions in the modern piano repertoire. 288pp. 8⅜ × 11¼. (Available in U.S. only) 25689-8 Pa. **$11.95**

GYMNOPÉDIES, GNOSSIENNES AND OTHER WORKS FOR PIANO, Erik Satie. The largest Satie collection of piano works yet published, 17 in all, reprinted from the original French editions. 176pp. 9 × 12. (Not available in France or Germany) 25978-1 Pa. **$8.95**

TWENTY SHORT PIECES FOR PIANO (Sports et Divertissements), Erik Satie. French master's brilliant thumbnail sketches—verbal and musical—of various outdoor sports and amusements. English translations, 20 illustrations. Rare, limited 1925 edition. 48pp. 12 × 8⅞. (Not available in France or Germany) 24365-6 Pa. **$5.95**

COMPLETE PRELUDES, IMPROMPTUS AND VALSES-CAPRICES, Gabriel Fauré. Eighteen elegantly wrought piano works in authoritative editions. Only one-volume collection. 144pp. 9 × 12. (Not available in France or Germany) 25789-4 Pa. **$8.95**

PIANO MUSIC OF BÉLA BARTÓK, Series I, Béla Bartók. New, definitive Archive Edition incorporating composer's corrections. Includes *Funeral March* from *Kossuth, Fourteen Bagatelles*, Bartók's break to modernism. 167pp. 9 × 12. (Available in U.S. only) 24108-4 Pa. **$10.95**

PIANO MUSIC OF BÉLA BARTÓK, Series II, Béla Bartók. Second in the Archie Edition incorporating composer's corrections. 85 short pieces *For Children, Two Elegies, Two Rumanian Dances*, etc. 192pp. 9 × 12. (Available in U.S. only) 24109-2 Pa. **$10.95**

FRENCH PIANO MUSIC, AN ANTHOLOGY, Isidor Phillipp (ed.). 44 complete works, 1670–1905, by Lully, Couperin, Rameau, Alkan, Saint-Saëns, Delibes, Bizet, Godard, many others; favorites, lesser-known examples, but all top quality. 188pp. 9 × 12. (Not available in France or Germany) 23381-2 Pa. **$9.95**

NINETEENTH-CENTURY EUROPEAN PIANO MUSIC: Unfamiliar Masterworks, John Gillespie (ed.). Difficult-to-find études, toccatas, polkas, impromptus, waltzes, etc., by Albéniz, Bizet, Chabrier, Fauré, Smetana, Richard Strauss, Wagner and 16 other composers. 62 pieces. 343pp. 9 × 12. (Not available in France or Germany) 23447-9 Pa. **$15.95**

RARE MASTERPIECES OF RUSSIAN PIANO MUSIC: Eleven Pieces by Glinka, Balakirev, Glazunov and Others, edited by Dmitry Feofanov. Glinka's *Prayer*, Balakirev's *Reverie*, Liapunov's *Transcendental Etude, Op. 11, No. 10*, and eight others—full, authoritative scores from Russian texts. 144pp. 9 × 12. 24659-0 Pa. **$8.95**

NINETEENTH-CENTURY AMERICAN PIANO MUSIC, edited by John Gillespie. 40 pieces by 27 American composers: Gottschalk, Victor Herbert, Edward MacDowell, William Mason, Ethelbert Nevin, others. 323pp. 9 × 12. 23602-1 Pa. **$14.95**

PIANO MUSIC, Louis M. Gottschalk. 26 pieces (including covers) by early 19th-century American genius. "Bamboula," "The Banjo," other Creole, Negro-based material, through elegant salon music. 301pp. 9¼ × 12. 21683-7 Pa. **$12.95**

SOUSA'S GREAT MARCHES IN PIANO TRANSCRIPTION, John Philip Sousa. Playing edition includes: "The Stars and Stripes Forever," "King Cotton," "Washington Post," much more. 24 illustrations. 111pp. 9 × 12. 23132-1 Pa. **$6.95**

COMPLETE PIANO RAGS, Scott Joplin. All 38 piano rags by the acknowledged master of the form, reprinted from the publisher's original editions complete with sheet music covers. Introduction by David A. Jasen. 208pp. 9 × 12. 25807-6 Pa. **$9.95**

RAGTIME REDISCOVERIES, selected by Trebor Jay Tichenor. 64 unusual rags demonstrate diversity of style, local tradition. Original sheet music. 320pp. 9 × 12. 23776-1 Pa. **$11.95**

RAGTIME RARITIES, edited by Trebor J. Tichenor. 63 tuneful, rediscovered piano rags by 51 composers (or teams). Does not duplicate selections in *Classic Piano Rags* (Dover, 20469-3). 305pp. 9 × 12. 23157-7 Pa. **$12.95**

CLASSIC PIANO RAGS, selected with an introduction by Rudi Blesh. Best ragtime music (1897–1922) by Scott Joplin, James Scott, Joseph F. Lamb, Tom Turpin, nine others. 364pp. 9 × 12. 20469-3 Pa. **$14.95**

RAGTIME GEMS: Original Sheet Music for 25 Ragtime Classics, edited by David A. Jasen. Includes original sheet music and covers for 25 rags, including three of Scott Joplin's finest: *Searchlight Rag, Rose Leaf Rag* and *Fig Leaf Rag*. 122pp. 9 × 12. 25248-5 Pa. **$7.95**

NOCTURNES AND BARCAROLLES FOR SOLO PIANO, Gabriel Fauré. 12 nocturnes and 12 barcarolles reprinted from authoritative French editions. 208pp. 9⅜ × 12¼. (Not available in France or Germany) 27955-3 Pa. **$10.95**

PRELUDES AND FUGUES FOR PIANO, Dmitry Shostakovich. 24 Preludes, Op. 34 and 24 Preludes and Fugues, Op. 87. Reprint of Gosudarstvennoe Izdatel'stvo Muzyka, Moscow, ed. 288pp. 8⅜ × 11. (Available in U.S. only) 26861-6 Pa. **$12.95**

FAVORITE WALTZES, POLKAS AND OTHER DANCES FOR SOLO PIANO, Johann Strauss, Jr. Blue Danube, Tales from Vienna Woods, many other best-known waltzes and other dances. 160pp. 9 × 12. 27851-4 Pa. **$9.95**

SELECTED PIANO WORKS FOR FOUR HANDS, Franz Schubert. 24 separate pieces (16 most popular titles): Three Military Marches, Lebensstürme, Four Polonaises, Four Ländler, etc. Rehearsal numbers added. 273pp. 9 × 12. 23529-7 Pa. **$11.95**

Dover Orchestral Scores

THREE ORCHESTRAL WORKS IN FULL SCORE: Academic Festival Overture, Tragic Overture and Variations on a Theme by Joseph Haydn, **Johannes Brahms.** Reproduced from the authoritative Breitkopf & Härtel edition three of Brahms's great orchestral favorites. Editor's commentary in German and English. 112pp. 9⅜ × 12¼.
24637-X Pa. **$8.95**

COMPLETE CONCERTI IN FULL SCORE, Johannes Brahms. Piano Concertos Nos. 1 and 2; Violin Concerto, Op. 77; Concerto for Violin and Cello, Op. 102. Definitive Breitkopf & Härtel edition. 352pp. 9⅜ × 12¼.
24170-X Pa. **$14.95**

COMPLETE SYMPHONIES IN FULL SCORE, Robert Schumann. No. 1 in B-flat Major, Op. 38 ("Spring"); No. 2 in C Major, Op. 61; No. 3 in E Flat Major, Op. 97 ("Rhenish"); and No. 4 in D Minor, Op. 120. Breitkopf & Härtel editions. Study score. 416pp. 9⅜ × 12¼.
24013-4 Pa. **$17.95**

GREAT WORKS FOR PIANO AND ORCHESTRA IN FULL SCORE, Robert Schumann. Collection of three superb pieces for piano and orchestra, including the popular Piano Concerto in A Minor. Breitkopf & Härtel edition. 183pp. 9⅜ × 12¼.
24340-0 Pa. **$9.95**

THE PIANO CONCERTOS IN FULL SCORE, Frédéric Chopin. The authoritative Breitkopf & Härtel full-score edition in one volume of Piano Concertos No. 1 in E Minor and No. 2 in F Minor. 176pp. 9 × 12.
25835-1 Pa. **$9.95**

THE PIANO CONCERTI IN FULL SCORE, Franz Liszt. Available in one volume the Piano Concerto No. 1 in E-flat Major and the Piano Concerto No. 2 in A Major—are among the most studied, recorded and performed of all works for piano and orchestra. 144pp. 9 × 12.
25221-3 Pa. **$8.95**

SYMPHONY NO. 8 IN G MAJOR, OP. 88, SYMPHONY NO. 9 IN E MINOR, OP. 95 ("NEW WORLD") IN FULL SCORE, Antonín Dvořák. Two celebrated symphonies by the great Czech composer, the Eighth and the immensely popular Ninth, "From the New World" in one volume. 272pp. 9 × 12.
24749-X Pa. **$12.95**

FOUR ORCHESTRAL WORKS IN FULL SCORE: Rapsodie Espagnole, Mother Goose Suite, Valses Nobles et Sentimentales, and Pavane for a Dead Princess, Maurice Ravel. Four of Ravel's most popular orchestral works, reprinted from original full-score French editions. 240pp. 9⅜ × 12¼. (Not available in France or Germany)
25962-5 Pa. **$11.95**

DAPHNIS AND CHLOE IN FULL SCORE, Maurice Ravel. Definitive full-score edition of Ravel's rich musical setting of a Greek fable by Longus is reprinted here from the original French edition. 320pp. 9⅜ × 12¼. (Not available in France or Germany) 25826-2 Pa. **$14.95**

THREE GREAT ORCHESTRAL WORKS IN FULL SCORE, Claude Debussy. Three favorites by influential modernist: *Prélude à l'Après-midi d'un Faune, Nocturnes,* and *La Mer.* Reprinted from early French editions. 279pp. 9 × 12.
24441-5 Pa. **$12.95**

SYMPHONY IN D MINOR IN FULL SCORE, César Franck. Superb, authoritative edition of Franck's only symphony, an often-performed and recorded masterwork of late French romantic style. 160pp. 9 × 12.
25373-2 Pa. **$9.95**

THE GREAT WALTZES IN FULL SCORE, Johann Strauss, Jr. Complete scores of eight melodic masterpieces: The Beautiful Blue Danube, Emperor Waltz, Tales of the Vienna Woods, Wiener Blut, four more. Authoritative editions. 336pp. 8⅜ × 11¼.
26009-7 Pa. **$13.95**

FOURTH, FIFTH AND SIXTH SYMPHONIES IN FULL SCORE, Peter Ilyitch Tchaikovsky. Complete orchestral scores of Symphony No. 4 in F minor, Op. 36; Symphony No. 5 in E minor, Op. 64; Symphony No. 6 in B minor, "Pathetique," Op. 74. Study score. Breitkopf & Härtel editions. 480pp. 9⅜ × 12¼.
23861-X Pa. **$19.95**

ROMEO AND JULIET OVERTURE AND CAPRICCIO ITALIEN IN FULL SCORE, Peter Ilyitch Tchaikovsky. Two of Russian master's most popular compositions in high quality, inexpensive reproduction. From authoritative Russian edition. 208pp. 8⅜ × 11½.
25217-5 Pa. **$9.95**

NUTCRACKER SUITE IN FULL SCORE, Peter Ilyitch Tchaikovsky. Among the most popular ballet pieces ever created—a complete, inexpensive, high-quality score to study and enjoy. 128pp. 9 × 12.
25379-1 Pa. **$7.95**

TONE POEMS, SERIES I: DON JUAN, TOD UND VERKLARUNG, and DON QUIXOTE, Richard Strauss. Three of the most often performed and recorded works in entire orchestral repertoire, reproduced in full score from original editions. Study score. 286pp. 9⅜ × 12¼. (Available in U.S. only)
23754-0 Pa. **$13.95**

TONE POEMS, SERIES II: TILL EULENSPIEGELS LUSTIGE STREICHE, ALSO SPRACH ZARATHUSTRA, and EIN HELDENLEBEN, Richard Strauss. Three important orchestral works, including very popular *Till Eulenspiegel's Merry Pranks,* reproduced in full score from original editions. Study score. 315pp. 9⅜ × 12¼. (Available in U.S. only)
23755-9 Pa. **$14.95**

DAS LIED VON DER ERDE IN FULL SCORE, Gustav Mahler. Mahler's masterpiece, a fusion of song and symphony, reprinted from the original 1912 Universal Edition. English translations of song texts. 160pp. 9 × 12.
25657-X Pa. **$8.95**

SYMPHONIES NOS. 1 AND 2 IN FULL SCORE, Gustav Mahler. Unabridged, authoritative Austrian editions of Symphony No. 1 in D Major ("Titan") and Symphony No. 2 in C Minor ("Resurrection"). 384pp. 8⅜ × 11.
25473-9 Pa. **$14.95**

SYMPHONIES NOS. 3 AND 4 IN FULL SCORE, Gustav Mahler. Two brilliantly contrasting masterworks—one scored for a massive ensemble, the other for small orchestra and soloist—reprinted from authoritative Viennese editions. 368pp. 9⅜ × 12¼. 26166-2 Pa. **$15.95**

SYMPHONY NO. 8 IN FULL SCORE, Gustav Mahler. Superb authoritative edition of massive, complex "Symphony of a Thousand." Scored for orchestra, eight solo voices, double chorus, boys' choir and organ. Reprint of Izdatel'stvo "Muzyka," Moscow, edition. Translation of texts. 272pp. 9⅜ × 12¼.
26022-4 Pa. **$12.95**

THE FIREBIRD IN FULL SCORE (Original 1910 Version), Igor Stravinsky. Handsome, inexpensive edition of modern masterpiece, renowned for brilliant orchestration, glowing color. Authoritative Russian edition. 176pp. 9⅜ × 12¼. (Available in U.S. only)
25535-2 Pa. **$9.95**

PETRUSHKA IN FULL SCORE: Original Version, Igor Stravinsky. The definitive full-score edition of Stravinsky's masterful score for the great Ballets Russes 1911 production of *Petrushka.* 160pp. 9⅜ × 12¼. (Available in U.S. only)
25680-4 Pa. **$9.95**

THE RITE OF SPRING IN FULL SCORE, Igor Stravinsky. A reprint of the original full-score edition of the most famous musical work of the 20th century, created as a ballet score for Diaghilev's Ballets Russes. 176pp. 9⅜ × 12¼. (Available in U.S. only)
25857-2 Pa. **$9.95**

---

*Available from your music dealer or write for **free** Music Catalog to* **Dover Publications, Inc., Dept. MUBI, 31 East 2nd Street, Mineola, N.Y. 11501.**